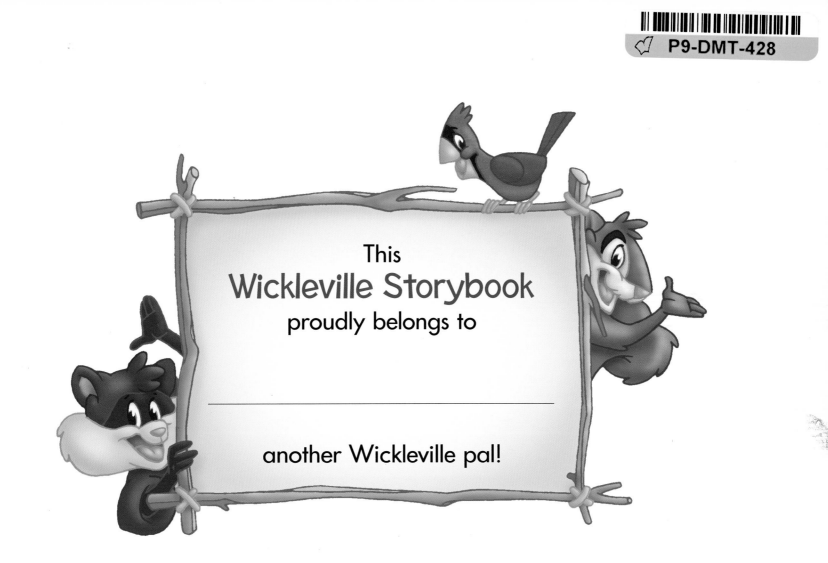

This
Wickleville Storybook
proudly belongs to

_____

another Wickleville pal!

Shelly's Race
©2000 by TREND enterprises, Inc.
Wickleville Woods™ is the registered trademark of TREND enterprises, Inc.

Printed in the United States of America

Lynae Wingate, John R. Kober – Editors

Library of Congress Catalog Card Number: 99-69467

ISBN 1-889319-74-0

10 9 8 7 6 5 4 3 2

Shelly's Race

by Jeffrey Sculthorp

Illustrations by Lorin Walter

WICKLEVILLE WOODS

TREND enterprises, Inc.

It was the day of Wickleville Woods' 10-mile run!

Shelly the turtle entered the big race just for fun.

She knew she might not win as she wished the others well.

Then she stepped to the start line and adjusted her shell.

When the starting flag waved, the runners ran fast.

Shelly the turtle was already the last.

Fifi la Fox started with amazing speed.

It was not a surprise that she had the lead.

The finish was close! The animals shouted a cheer.

Fifi la Fox was first; second came Daphne the deer.

All the animals finished, except for one.

Shelly the turtle had just barely begun.

She was getting so tired, but she happily said,

"I'm glad to be racing, though I was never ahead."

"I'm trying as hard as I can. I'm giving it my best.

I can't help it that I'm not as fast as all of the rest."

"I'm joining the fun, and though I won't win first place,

I'm just proud to run in the big 10-mile race."

Many hours later Shelly came into sight.

To cross the finish line she had to race all night.

The animals were there as she finished the race.

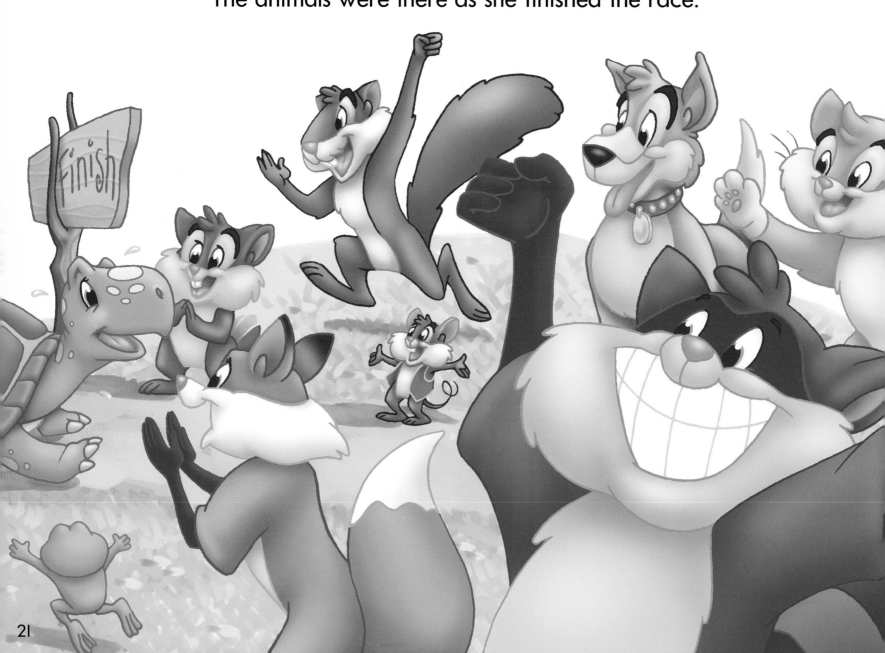

It was the next morning when she came in last place.

Fifi la Fox was proud, along with all the rest.

Shelly tried so hard and gave it her very best.

All the animals were happy because in the end...

Shelly won a trophy for being the **Number One Friend.**

The End